Also by Amelia Littlewood
Death at the Netherfield Park Ball
The Mystery of the Indian Diadem
The Peculiar Doctor Barnabus
The Apparition at Rosing's Park
The Shadow of Moriarty
The Adventure of the King's Portrait

Copyright © 2018 Amelia Littlewood
All rights reserved.
Published by Cyanide Publishing
www.cyanidepublishing.com

First edition
No part of this book may be used or reproduced in any manner whatsoever without the prior written permission of the publisher, except in the case of brief quotations embodied in reviews.

This is a work of fiction. Names, characters, businesses, places, events and incidents are either the products of the author's imagination or used in a fictitious manner. Any resemblance to actual persons, living or dead, or actual events is purely coincidental.

ISBN: 9781980548522

FROM THE JANE AUSTEN NOVEL
Pride & Prejudice

The Adventure
of the King's
Portrait

A Sherlock Holmes & Elizabeth Bennet Mystery

AMELIA LITTLEWOOD

CYANIDE PUBLISHING

Chapter One:
A Detective's Obsession

I had, in my time with Mr. Holmes, come to both appreciate his virtues and grow accustomed to his flaws. There were things about him that I now took for granted and adjusted my behavior for without conscious thought, whereas others would be surprised or appalled and would inevitably make a disparaging comment. My mother was certainly one of those people.

We had reached an uneasy truce, Mother and me. She still didn't like the idea of me throwing myself into danger and possibly damaging my reputation in spending time with someone like Mr. Holmes, a man who is outside of the landed gentry and who regularly deals with the homeless and the criminal element. It did not matter at all to me who Mr. Holmes had to interact with in the course of obtaining information for his cases, nor did I particularly care if my reputation was damaged.

It was reckless of me, I know, but I had found a real purpose in my life in helping the people that came to Mr. Holmes for assistance. Before I had met Mr. Holmes, my life had been rather boring, although I hadn't had the courage to admit as much to myself. I had nothing to stimulate my intellect. I had my dear friend Charlotte and of course my sister Jane, the person in the world to whom I was closest, but I knew their companionship was temporary in a manner of speaking. As soon as we all married, we would be inevitably separated. And while I did love their company, talking about who had married whom, who had given birth, and so on could only carry my mind so far.

With Mr. Holmes, I was finally getting to stretch my mind and create an impact in people's lives. I had purpose. It also enabled me to stay in London near my dear Jane and assist her through her trying pregnancy and now being a young mother. I was no longer stuck at Longbourn, whiling away the hours with books, stagnating and yearning desperately for something, anything, to come along and break the state of mental limbo that I was in. Now I was truly living life.

I knew that Mother would never truly understand this. I had, through talks with others, come to understand her concern for me more and did try to act in deference to it. But I would not stop what had become my chief joy in life.

And so it was that in the afternoons, after morning calls were paid, I usually found myself at 221b Baker Street. I did try to avoid calls when I could, but I was unable to fully escape them, especially now that the rest of my family was temporarily in Jane's London home. Mother and Father would soon be going home, for Father hated London. There were far too many people for his taste. And where Father went, Mother went. I had made some observations of late, including the pinched look around Mother's mouth and the less care she took in her wardrobe, and knew that it was because she was worried for Father's health. Once there was a time when she would have begged him to let her stay in London, even without him. Now she simply planned to follow him back home to Longbourn without complaint.

Personally, I had higher hopes for my father's health, but Mother is always fancying herself sick in some way and so sees it in others as well.

My younger sisters, however, would be staying. Mother would not be dissuaded on that count. I had introduced Kitty and Lydia, my two youngest sisters, to the sweet and delightful Miss Georgiana Darcy, and the three had come to a close friendship. It was due in part, I believe, to Miss Georgiana and Lydia's having both been temporarily in the clutches of the unscrupulous Mr. Wickham, a rake who had met an unpleasant but—in my mind at least—not entirely undeserved end.

The three being so close, and with the London season upon us, Mother insisted that Kitty and Lydia make their official debut with the help of Jane and Mr. Bingley, my brother-in-law, so that my sisters might make something of themselves. Mr. Bingley had five thousand a year, and I believe Mother's hope was that her two younger daughters would make even better matches of it.

My middle sister Mary was also staying, although I could not rightfully blame her for our sudden influx of social calls that forced me to either stay home and help Jane receive them or go out on Jane's behalf or as a chaperone to Kitty, Lydia, and Miss Georgiana. Mary stayed in London because she wished to study, as surreptitiously and extensively as she might, in matters of law and the classics.

We might have purposefully failed to mention that to Mother when it was suggested that Mary, too, should stay in London.

And so it was that I found my time with Mr. Holmes shorter than usual. I confess, although I felt it shallow of me, that I hoped my sisters would soon find a husband just as my mother hoped, so that my life with Jane might return to its usual tranquility and I could devote the entirety of my time to Mr. Holmes rather than snatching it when I could.

I was certain that Mr. Holmes would remark upon it when I entered his flat, but to my surprise, he did not even greet me. Mr. Holmes was not a man known for his geniality or his sense of manners, but I had steadily been working with him on the idea that in order to keep getting clients one must put on at least a show of some consideration, which included greeting people when they entered one's apartment.

But there was no, "Ah, Miss Bennet," followed by an observation or an introduction on a case he was working. Instead, I found him staring at the many pictures and scribbled notes on his wall, the one that I had secretly come to call the Spider's Web for the little bits of red string crisscrossing it.

In truth, I did not always believe in this Moriarty we were chasing. It sounded fantastical. But more worrisome than the reality of a supposed master criminal was how obsessive my friend was becoming about it. Could he no longer notice or care when I entered?

"Mr. Holmes," I said, alerting him to my presence.

He continued to stare at the wall for a moment, then cleared his throat and turned to look at me. I saw at once that he was not sleeping as he should. Not that Mr. Holmes ever cared much for his personal health—the amount he smoked his pipe spoke to that. "Miss Bennet." He looked me up and down. "Still forced to attend the London Season, I see."

"Jane cannot attend, what with the baby still so young." Jane had, despite my desperate fears, recovered nicely from her pregnancy and had delivered a healthy baby boy, named after my father. But a baby has demands and Jane, bless her sweet nature, would not give him over to a wet nurse so that she might attend balls.

"And have your sisters succeeded yet in finding husbands?" Mr. Holmes asked, and then immediately corrected himself. "No, I see they have not."

"I am getting too much sleep for that," I said, deducing that he had noticed the lack of circles under my eyes. If either Kitty or Lydia had been proposed to, I should not have gotten a wink of sleep for all the excited dashing about and squealing that would have gone on.

"Precisely." Mr. Holmes then turned back to his wall.

I held in my sigh. "Mr. Holmes, you have spent the last month staring at those papers. They will not transform into new information before your eyes."

"And yet, one must be persistent in the hunt," Mr. Holmes countered.

"Did no one ever tell you that the key to success in life is moderation?" I replied. "Mr. Holmes, please. Allow me to make you some tea."

I had never known how to make tea, or anything else, or clean, before I had met Mr. Holmes. There were always servants to take care of that for me. Now I knew how to make tea, and cook a little, and clean almost anything.

"I have no need of it," Mr. Holmes replied, waving me off.

"You certainly do," I told him. "Mr. Holmes, I am concerned. Your obsession with this person—who we still have yet to see in the flesh—is not healthy. How many cases have you turned away because of this?"

"You are not my mother, the last I checked," Mr. Holmes said.

Once, such a comment would have insulted me. But I had grown used to arguing with Mr. Holmes during the course of our acquaintance. He could not so easily send me off into a huff or intimidate me with his blunt manner. "No, but I am your friend and, I should hope, a person possessing common sense. Come now. Stepping away and working upon another case will keep your faculties sharp. I think a change of pace might even do you good, you can come back and look at this with fresh eyes."

There was silence for a moment, and then Mr. Holmes said, "Miss Bennet, do I seem mentally sound to you?"

I paused. "What would bring on such a question?" Mr. Holmes was the most intelligent and sane man that I knew. Whatever he lacked in social skills he made up for in sense and logic. Mr. Holmes did not know much of the soft things in life. Indeed, he scorned them, rejected romance and sentiment, and I had never once seen him so much as glance at a poem or stop to observe a pretty view. Lord Byron should have been appalled at Mr. Holmes, and I knew that the feeling would have been mutual.

Mr. Holmes gestured at the wall. "This. You say I am growing obsessed. Is that not one of the signs of mental imbalance?"

"I think it is merely your sense of determination," I told him."

"Perhaps. But I do fear that I am overestimating this character. I wonder if I have simply made up his accomplishments."

I did not think Mr. Holmes would go so far as to make up an enemy for himself, but I could see why Mr. Holmes should fear that. He was often bored and would embark on the most insane experiments in order to occupy his mind. One time I came to find a human skull sitting on the table surrounded by vials with which he was coating the skull. Another time I entered the apartment only to gag from the awful smell and be told that Mr. Holmes was conducting a study in organ decay.

When I say that being Mr. Holmes's partner is not for the faint of stomach, I do mean that literally.

It was not a stretch, I supposed, that to try and stimulate his mind, Mr. Holmes would wish for a master criminal. Someone on the opposite side of the law who was his equal, with whom he could finally engage in proper mental chess. It was appealing, and while I did not doubt Mr. Holmes's sanity, I could see why he would doubt his own and wonder if his wishful thinking was impairing his judgment.

"Well," I said, "As you cannot learn anything new, perhaps it is time to set it aside for now. Many great mathematicians have had to set their figures aside for a time and I dare say we stretch our minds just as they do. I can ask around among my acquaintances at the balls and see if anyone is in need of our assistance. A few new cases away from this matter will be what's best."

"I suppose you are right," Mr. Holmes replied.

I could not resist smiling. "Is the great detective actually conceding that I am right?"

Mr. Holmes gave me a stern look. "So long as you do not rub it in."

I was glad that I could get my friend back into better humor, but before I could further bolster his spirits, Mrs. Hudson entered. "Mr. Holmes? Miss Bennet?"

"Yes," we answered at once.

"You have a visitor." Mrs. Hudson, for once, looked shaken. "A very important one."

"How important?" I asked, for in Mr. Holmes's mind a person's importance depended upon the complexity of their case and not their social status.

Before Mrs. Hudson could reply, a man brushed past her into the room. Instinctively, I went down upon my knees, bowing my head, for I felt a simple curtsy would not do in such a situation. I had not met the man himself before but I had seen his portrait and heard of him, just as I had heard of and seen portraits of many royals.

It was the King of Bohemia.

Chapter Two:
The Misplaced Portrait

"Please, dear lady, don't make a fuss on my account," the king said.

The discrete reader will no doubt note that I am not using the king's precise name—in fact, the reader might very well wonder whether it was the king of Bohemia at all, or if it was not another member of royalty altogether. As a woman who seeks through Mr. Holmes to both exercise my own mind and help others, and I cannot do the former and go directly against the latter if I am careless with client privacy, I'm sure readers will forgive me for choosing a country at random and merely addressing our client as 'the king'.

I quickly stood but was unsure of how next to behave. A member of royalty, coming here—it was unbelievable. In fact, I discreetly pinched myself to make sure that I was still awake.

Mr. Holmes, of course, did nothing of the sort. He didn't even bow, so far as I could tell. Instead he turned and looked the king directly in the eye. While it was still obvious, at least in my mind, when I was looking someone up and down in order to observe them, Mr. Holmes managed to take in every aspect of a person while either looking them directly in the eye the entire time or not even appearing to look at them at all.

"Would you care for some tea?" I asked. While others have been known to comment upon the stereotypes of the British with a condescending manner, I must say that when one is in the middle of a social crisis, I dare anyone to think of something that will better help to clear the air and soothe everyone's nerves than offering some tea.

After all, even if the offer of tea is refused, it's usually enough to jumpstart a conversation when needed. The king looked at me and blinked for a moment, as if in confusion, then gave an apologetic smile. "I'm afraid I don't have time for such pleasantries. I've taken care that nobody know I'm here, but the court will soon miss me if I stay for too long."

"Of course," I said, taking over the conversation since I knew Mr. Holmes would not want to deal with such conventions. "Why don't you get down to the matter at hand then. Please, sit if you would like." I gestured to one of the chairs.

"This is, as I'm sure you must both already guess, a matter of some urgency and discretion," the king said. "You are probably wondering at my coming here myself, rather than employing someone else—"

"But you have a matter of such delicacy that you cannot entrust to anyone else," Mr. Holmes finished.

The king stared at Mr. Holmes in fascination. "Yes, it is true."

"A matter regarding something personal, no doubt, rather than a matter of state," Mr. Holmes went on.

"Well, yes, but how on earth did you come by such a deduction?"

Mr. Holmes looked at me and I saw that he wished for me to answer the question. I tried to speak calmly, as I would to any other client who came to the flat. "You allowed yourself to be seen by our landlady," I said. "While Mrs. Hudson is a most respectable woman, you were willing to chance a random Londoner of the lower classes seeing your face over sending a servant to disclose the case to Mr. Holmes. In this case, the matter could not be something of state, because your advisors and allies would need to know of it—rather it is a matter of personal discretion, and something serious enough that you would rather have a random woman telling her friends that she saw a king before you handed such dangerous information to a subordinate in your household."

The king looked at me with a kind of reluctant respect, and I saw Mr. Holmes give one of his tiny, almost humorless smiles. "Miss Bennet here is my associate. You can say anything in front of her just as you would in front of me. She possesses admirable deducting skills."

Our visitor seemed unsure what to say to that, and in the end bowed to me. "Well, then, I suppose I should better explain myself. Some five years ago I made the acquaintance of a young adventuress by the name of Irene Adler."

To use the word 'adventuress' I found rather damning. It was a polite term used to describe a woman who operated outside the bounds of society, generally by serving as a courtesan of sorts to rich and noble men. Yet, I had heard that name before.

"Miss Adler is an opera singer," I said. "A contralto." I remembered her for Jane loved the opera, and true contraltos are rare and greatly prized by operatic composers for their rich, lower voices. "I believe, if my memory serves, she was born in New Jersey in the Americas, and at one point served as the Prima Donna for the Warsaw Imperial Opera."

"Your knowledge is accurate and commendable," the king replied. "She was, in fact, the lead at the Warsaw company when I was also there. She has since been to other companies and is a well-traveled young lady, never settling down for long. It was as though the moment I learned of her address but she was off somewhere new. Now, I hear, she has settled more permanently in London at the Royal Opera House as their premiere star."

"I am given to understand," Mr. Holmes said, "That you have in some way given the lady some token of yours that she can use to blackmail you."

"Yes, precisely, that is it," the king said, nodding. "You are as accurate as my associates proclaimed, Mr. Holmes."

I had to admit, the king was a rather good-looking gentleman. I could understand why, five years earlier when he was more youthful, an opera singer would be eager to fall for such a man. He was not to

17

my tastes, but he fit the tastes of many women I knew, including those of my youngest sisters.

"But what was your indiscretion?" I asked, not out of morbid curiosity but out of a desire to understand.

"What my associate means," Mr. Holmes added, "Is that, was there a secret marriage of any kind between the two of you? Anything that might bind you to one another legally?"

"Oh good heavens, no," the king proclaimed. "It was not at all of that nature. I have done many a foolish thing in my time, Mr. Holmes, but my stupidity never went as far as that."

"Then why worry about her?" I asked. This was the reason for my questioning—if there was nothing to bind the two of them legally to one another then why should the king worry? His people would be more willing to believe a man in a high position than they would a woman who was an artist. The public went to the opera and loved it but at the end of the day, actors of all kinds were still seen as inherently base and scandalous in their inclinations.

"There are—letters, that is…"

"Those can easily be faked," Mr. Holmes replied. "As can your royal seal. Even if it is on your private notepaper, such things can be stolen or imitated."

"It is not that." The king looked almost ashamed, and I realized that he was embarrassed. His eyes flicked over to me for a moment. "There is a photograph… which I had sent to the lady, with my handwriting upon the back... which shows my figure in a most indelicate light."

I realized the reason for the king's embarrassment and felt heat rise to my face. "I hope you will not take this as berating you," I said, "For I would never seek to rise above my station is such a manner, but I hope your Majesty has realized the extent of foolishness that was."

"I am, unfortunately, painfully aware of my youthful idiocy. I remember when I sent it to her I urged her in the note upon the back to use it to think of me while she was away on tour." The king sighed. "I thought then only of the pleasures of the moment. I was not yet risen to my current position of responsibility."

Personally, I thought it quite unfair for the man to send such a piece of damning evidence to a woman only to then blame her for having it five years later. "Are you certain that she does still have this photograph?" I asked, for five years was a long time. My sister Jane had, when she was but fifteen, a suitor that Mother was convinced would propose marriage. He didn't, thank heavens, but he did leave with Jane some tokens of affection such as a letter and a ribbon. Jane held onto them for a short while, but then disposed of them, giving the ribbon to Charlotte and burning the letter.

Only the most dire and passionate of loves, I was sure, could compel a woman to keep something of that nature for five years, especially when it would ruin her if discovered. Never mind that she had not asked for it, she was implicated by having it.

"You are to be married, are you not?" Mr. Holmes interjected.

I was not at all certain where he was going with this, but I trusted him enough to stay quiet.

"Yes," the king replied. "To a lady of a most delicate nature and from a very pious family. If I were marrying into certain other royal families I am sure that a youthful dalliance such as this would go unnoticed, but I would be treated with horror and disdain if my fiancée and her family were to learn of this."

I was aware that royal marriages were almost always political in nature. It was not love that guided the king's fears but rather politics—he must need an alliance with the royal family of the woman he was marrying, and endangering that was akin to weakening his country and endangering his kingdom. I wondered briefly which had the most powerful hold, the ties of love, or the ties of a kingdom's prosperity and safety?

"And this Miss Adler has threatened to send the photograph to your intended and her family, or to otherwise make it public?"

"She said that she would make it public the day that my engagement was made public, which is only three days from now. I arranged to come to London so that I could employ your services."

"But are you sure that she will go through with it?" I asked. "It could be that she only wants money or jewelry or something in order to compensate her, or that she is making a false attempt in order to draw you back to her."

"If it were any other woman, I should think so as well," the king admitted. "But not so Miss Adler. She has a soul of steel. She has the face of the most beautiful of women, and the mind of the most resolute of men. If she has promised something, then it shall happen."

"In that case we have but three days." Mr. Holmes nodded. "I shall trouble you with the fee when the case has been solved. Until then, if you will allow it, my associate and I shall set to work."

The king bowed. "Thank you. If you are able to obtain that photograph from her, I shall be most in your debt."

With that he bowed again as a farewell and left the room.

Chapter Three:
A Trip to the Opera

"Well," I said, and stopped, for I did not know what else to say.

"I see that the presence of such an illustrious visitor has you on the rocks," Mr. Holmes noted in a wry tone. "But I must commend you, Miss Bennet, for keeping your head as you usually do. I have known too many men and women who fawn over their supposed betters at the first opportunity."

"I have faced the likes of Lady Catherine de Bourgh," I reminded him. "After that, it should take more than an irresponsible monarch to shake me."

Mr. Holmes chuckled, amused at my joke and well remembering the draconian attitude of the lady in question. "Indeed. Well, it seems to me, Miss Bennet, that you are to chaperone your sisters to a very different sort of event tonight."

"What do you mean?" I asked. Had Mr. Holmes observed or overheard something that I had not in regards to London society? I knew that he regularly paid various servants and homeless persons around London in order to be informed about all manner of goings-on.

"I mean only that you are to take them to the opera," Mr. Holmes said. "For that is where Miss Adler will be tonight. It wouldn't do for me to be seen there but it would be natural that a lady of your station should wish to educate her younger siblings on such culture."

It did in fact make a great deal of sense. "And what shall I learn from watching her from a box?" I asked.

"I'm certain you can find a way to arrange an in-person meeting with her," Mr. Holmes replied.

I was never one to back down from a challenge. Whether this was a virtue or a fault depended upon who you were asking. My mother, and I am certain some people I knew such as Mr. Darcy, would be eager to name it a fault. But when it came to solving a crime, I tended to look upon it as a virtue. After all, if one is not determined, then how can one solve the mystery?

To my surprise, Kitty and Lydia were open to the idea of attending the opera. "Many balls won't start until it gets out anyhow," Lydia said. "And there we can see others in their boxes and they shall see us!"

Part of me despaired at the idea of my sisters using the time at the opera to look for eligible men rather than paying attention to the fine art on display, but as it would distract them from realizing what my true purpose was, I could not complain too much. Mr. Bingley elected to stay home, and Jane could not even think of going in case the baby needed her. I offered to Mary as well, but she expressed distaste at the idea of being trapped in a small box with Kitty and Lydia for so long a time. Lydia had become much better in the time since her incident with Wickham, but her energy was still too much for Mary to handle.

I invited Miss Georgiana to accompany us as well, upon Kitty and Lydia's insistence, despite my misgiving that Mr. Darcy might come along. While we had agreed upon a kind of truce in our mutual antagonism, I feared that he would interfere with my sleuthing plans.

Fortunately, Mr. Darcy did not wish to join his sister in accompanying us, and so I was to chaperone the three young ladies. Kitty was the most excited to meet the other theatregoers in the lobby and during the intermissions. Georgiana was happy to meet people but was not one to let her excitement show so readily or let it control her. Lydia was, as usual since her encounter with Mr. Wickham, nervous. I took care to be near her at all times so that she might have a feeling of safety as she met new people, especially men. While Georgiana had been tricked by Mr. Wickham, he had never touched her or attempted to take advantage of her physically as he had with Lydia, and so it was understandable that Georgiana was more easily able to recover and find joy in crowds of people again.

I settled myself with the three girls in the box and we waited for the opera to begin. I had brought with me a pair of glasses so that I could easily observe the stage and the players.

It was quickly apparent to me that this Miss Adler was a wonder. Firstly, I must admit that her former companion was not amiss when he said she had the face of the loveliest of women. I myself was astounded at her looks, and I could see when I trained my glasses upon the men in the boxes that they, too, were dumbstruck.

Personally, however, it was her singing that held me. She was a highly talented singer and given that she was a true contralto it was obvious that the composers had been eager to showcase her specifically. She carried herself with grace and power, and I found myself a little under her spell the way any audience member is when being entertained by a true artist.

Of course, I reminded myself, it could all be an act. She was a performer, after all. The bewitching creature on stage could turn out to be a selfish and uncaring person in her personal life. I was curious to see what Miss Adler would be like off stage when she was herself, and not playing a part.

I was patient all throughout the opera. It was easy, seeing as it entertained me. It was a retelling of Greek myth, as many popular operas are, and the three younger girls were also thoroughly entertained by the tragic romance and the depictions of fights featuring both heroic demigods and dastardly villains.

By the opera's end it was easy for me to convince the girls I had to powder my nose while I left them in the care of some acquaintances. Several young men were in the group and I knew that my sisters, at least, would not notice any time passing until I returned. Miss Georgiana was a more observant girl, but I trusted her to not be suspicious of me or ask questions.

I made my way quickly to the side door of the theatre, where I observed many of the chorus already departing. I stood to the side and listened carefully to their chatter. One of them seemed the kind of man to always have a new lady friend: I observed upon him both expensive cologne and a whiff of women's perfume, and he had done himself up well except for the unbuttoning of some buttons at his collar, exposing a bit of his collarbones to help him straddle the line between being rakish and gentlemanly. Finally, in his coat buttonhole I saw pinned a small pink flower—undoubtedly put there by a lady of some kind.

As he walked by me he took out his pocket watch and I quickly looked down to see engraved upon it, *To Edward, with love, A.*

After the group had thinned out I quickly knocked on the door that led into the stage area. It was opened by a gruff looking gentleman, and I smiled and curtsied.

"I'm terribly sorry," I said, pitching my voice up and stuttering over my words, "But I'm looking for Edward, is he still about?"

"Somewhere, I'm sure." The man eyed me. "You must be the new friend of his."

I smiled as if to say that I was guilty as charged. The man sighed and opened the door further to let me in. "Don't dally, and tell him to hurry up and get out."

"Oh, of course, I'm quite sorry," I replied, stammering and looking quite nervous.

Now that I was backstage, I had to find Miss Adler before anyone else saw me and realized that I didn't belong there. I hurried through the darkened backstage area, being careful not to trip over lights and blocks of wood and set pieces and costumes, great piles of detritus that seemed to be haphazardly arranged every which-way. I should have thought that dealing with Mr. Holmes's scattered apartment would do something for my ability to handle mess, but this was something else entirely.

Once I picked my way across the back of the stage I was able to find the dressing rooms. It seemed that all the female chorus members shared one room, while all the male chorus members shared another. Then came a few individual dressing rooms for the stars. Conveniently, each room had the person's name on it—and thank goodness for that, because I certainly didn't want to draw attention to myself by just knocking on doors.

I disheveled myself a little, rumpling up my dress and letting loose a few curls of my hair, and then banged into Miss Adler's room.

"Oh my goodness!" I said, quickly closing the door behind me. "Oh—oh please, is it all right if I stay with you for a moment?"

Miss Adler was sitting on a chair in front of a table, clearly having been in the process of taking off her makeup. She was even more beautiful without it, for makeup on an operatic stage was meant to exaggerate one's features so that the actor could be seen even from far away. She had dark auburn hair and green eyes, a rare combination. "Are you all right?" she asked.

I could understand why the king had fallen for her. I made a quick sweep of the room—but of course she would not have the photograph here. Why keep it in a place that was so messy, where people could so easily go through your things? "I'm terribly sorry. I'm just trying to… well, it's awfully embarrassing."

"My specialty," Miss Adler replied. She indicated a small couch. "Sit, you look a fright."

"Oh, I know, I look awful," I moaned, patting my hair. "You must understand, I never do this, but my mother pressures me so and… well, when someone of such high status asks you can't really say no…"

Miss Adler raised an eyebrow, a shrewd look upon her face. "I take it your gentleman companion intended to use his opera box for things other than watching the opera?"

This was something I had learned from Mr. Holmes, which was that people would happily fill in the blanks if you simply started the sentence for them. They would supply you with the information that you needed—all you had to do was start out with the generalities, and their mind would leap to what, to them, was the most logical conclusion. Then you could just go along with whatever they said without having to make anything up yourself.

"Yes," I said, nodding. "Oh, dear, I don't know what to do, really I don't. I shall have to find another carriage home. And what if he's angry with me? Only—I know he won't propose and I could never—"

"Breathe," Miss Adler told me. She was looking at me kindly, with a kind of sad look in her eyes. "Trust me, you're in good company here. I well understand how men work. You give them a little courtesy and a little thoughtfulness and suddenly they think they can take whatever they please from you."

I nodded, and thought of the saddest thing I could: when Jane had been in labor and we had feared her dying.

It worked, causing tears to spring to my eyes, and I began to weep. Miss Adler sprung up at once, fetching a handkerchief and passing it to me. "I just don't know what to do," I cried.

"There, there, it will be all right," Miss Adler replied. She patted my shoulder comfortingly. "Why, I was in a similar situation to yourself. I was exchanging letters with a man… I attempted to dissuade him, but I could not risk offending him."

"What did you do about it?" I asked.

Miss Adler smiled at me. It wasn't a cold smile, but it was a sharp one. "I managed to suggest to him that a photograph of him for me would not go amiss."

"What could a photograph possibly do?" I asked. "You could have gotten a portrait of him any number of places."

"This was a photograph of a certain nature," Miss Adler replied.

I let my jaw drop a little and my eyes widen, feigning shock. "And did he give it to you?"

Miss Adler nodded. "I now had power over him. If he did something that could harm me, I could use it against him."

"That is very clever," I said, and I wasn't pretending at all when I said that. I could not help but sympathize with Miss Adler's position. It seemed to me that she had not genuinely cared for the king as he had for her and had attempted to dissuade him from pursuing her. In a way it was fair that she should have some kind of insurance over him.

However, her announcing to him that she would share the photograph the day that he made his engagement public prevented me from being completely on her side. What reason would she have to cause a national scandal?

I couldn't ask her about that, unfortunately, because that would mean divulging that I knew of her plan, which as far as she knew, only the king was aware of. I said nothing, and instead resolved to tell Mr. Holmes of what I had learned.

"Thank you for the idea," I said, smiling at her. "I should get back, before anyone notices… and I shall have to find a carriage home. You're really too kind."

"Not at all," Miss Adler replied. "We women must stick together. What is your name?"

"Miss Elizabeth Bennet," I said, for I saw no reason to lie. Perhaps it might prove useful for us to know one another. I could arrange for a social visit that way.

"I'm sure you've already recognized me but if not, I'm Miss Irene Adler." She helped me to my feet. "Be sure to let me know how you fare."

"Oh, I shall," I said, although I didn't mean it in the way that she thought. When this case was wrapped, I had a feeling that she would know more about my true nature than she did at the moment.

I bid Miss Adler adieu and found my way back to my three charges. They were being thoroughly entertained—and by entertained, I mean flirted with—by several young men. Mother, at least, would be delighted when she heard the news.

I gathered the three women up, much to their dismay, and escorted them home, dropping Miss Georgiana off at her place and then making sure Lydia and Kitty got to bed. I made sure to stop by Jane's room—she was awake with the baby, for he had a tendency to fuss in the middle of the night, and I was able to relate to her all about the opera that she had missed.

If only it could always be this way, I thought—my family life and my work with Mr. Holmes balancing themselves out in so simple and easy a fashion.

As I was to learn in the morning, however, my personal and my detecting lives were about to intersect in a way I hadn't imagined.

Chapter Four:
Mary Lends a Hand

The next morning at breakfast there was much animated talk from Kitty and Lydia about the various men to whom they'd spoken. Between the opera and balls they were attending every night, I had to confess that even with my more realistic nature, it wouldn't be long before one or both of them was proposed to. Mother would be ecstatic. I, for one, cared only that they not rush into a marriage with a man who was all charm and no substance.

I endured it as best I could, but I was grateful when they departed to make calls for the day and silence fell over the house once more—I, for once, begged off, and since it was only calling I supposed that there wasn't too much trouble they could get into without me present. Jane was upstairs with the baby in the nursery, and Mary was in the library, as was her habit.

Mary had previously expressed a sympathy for my situation and an interest in my work, and I thought it might be pleasant for her if I was to tell her about our latest case. I was still unsure what to do about Mary, although I pretended that I was confident if only for her sake. When she had confided in me that she, too, found herself bored and longing for something more out of life, I admit I'd been caught by surprise. I'd always thought that Mary was content with her reading and banging away at the pianoforte. I had realized in that moment that I had sadly underestimated her.

That was something I was learning while working with Mr. Holmes—I had, unknown to myself until recently, the most damnable prideful streak.

Mary looked up upon my entrance and set her book aside as I sat down. "Is something the matter?" she asked.

It stung a little, for Mary to think that the only reason I would talk to her would be if something was wrong. "No, not at all. I only wanted to tell you a bit about the case I'm working on with Mr. Holmes. I thought it might hold some interest to you."

"Oh." Mary seemed surprised, but pleased, a slight blush crossing her cheeks. "I would—that is, yes. Thank you."

I sketched out the case for her, although like certain readers, Mary equally suspected that I had changed the country and perhaps even the rank of the royal gentleman in question. "If this gentleman is who I think he is, and not who you say he is," Mary said at last, "Then this is not the first scandal he has been involved with. His early days were reckless ones."

"How did you come to learn of such things?" I asked, curious.

"I have made it a pastime to read the paper and follow the movement of governments," Mary replied. "And I like to eavesdrop on the men at the balls. You know how Mother always made me go and I do detest dancing, but listening to the men discussing politics and law was very interesting."

"My dear Mary," I exclaimed, "I fear I've dreadfully underestimated you."

Mary gave me a small, pleased smile. "You would not be the first," she replied.

"What sort of scandals has he been involved in?" I asked.

"Nothing of the same nature as what you're describing to me," Mary answered. "A few years ago it was said that he had let some important papers regarding treaties be stolen and copied out under his nose. Of course they turned the household inside out to find out who had assisted in it, but they could find no evidence to blame it on anyone."

"Then news of this scandal would be disastrous," I said. "Even on its own it is enough to ruin his engagement, but after previous cases of carelessness, surely his advisors and other countries would be hesitant about having him in a powerful position."

"Yes." Mary nodded. "Of course, officially no one can do anything to him, but there are, as I'm sure you know in working with Mr. Holmes, other ways of getting rid of someone you consider to be a weak link."

"I wonder then," I said, "If someone else has not heard of the picture in Miss Adler's possession. When I spoke to her last night, she seemed to have it only as a weapon of self-defense. Yet the king told Mr. Holmes and me that she had, of her own accord, threatened to make the picture public on the day he announced his engagement. Why would she do that, unless someone had contacted her and asked her to make it worth her while?"

"You know, that sounds rather like a person whose name has been cropping up in conversation." Mary's eyes took on a conspiratorial gleam. "I have heard of him—I assume it is a him, that is—from time to time, but always when it was only two or three very important men in a group talking, and always in whispers."

My breath caught in my throat. It felt almost like too much of a coincidence, but Mr. Holmes had taught me that there was no such thing. "Is his name, by chance, Moriarty?"

Mary gasped. "Then you have heard of him as well?"

"More than that—he wished to intimidate Mr. Holmes and learn what he could about him, since Mr. Holmes has come to the attention of powerful people who seek his assistance. I think Moriarty felt that Mr. Holmes might threaten his business and so sought to scare Mr. Holmes off. He arranged for us to be attacked, but we managed to handle it nicely." I failed to mention to her that I had been kidnapped and nearly killed. I did not think it would be wise to scare my sister, especially when I was now hale and hearty and there was no reason to worry.

"That is unfortunate," Mary said. "From what I understand he has become a great concern for the Empire and other European governments."

She spoke with such confidence, as though she had no doubt as to her knowledge, that I was struck with a great wave of sadness. It was a pity that she was not born a boy, I thought. She would have made an excellent member of Parliament or a lawyer, or even as a member of the clergy if she wished. Her intellect and understanding of politics was being wasted, all because she was a woman.

Mary gave me an odd look. "What is it?"

I supposed that some of what I was thinking showed on my face. I knew that Mary would not welcome any pity or sympathy for her plight, so instead of telling her the truth I simply said, "You ought to come with me. You should be discussing this with Mr. Holmes. He will find it very useful."

I stood, and Mary followed me. If nothing else, I thought, this proved once and for all that Mr. Holmes was not losing his mind or obsessing over a phantom.

Mary was silent on our trip to 221b Baker Street. I observed her index finger quietly tracing a pattern in her skirt and saw that she kept her gaze out the window but pointed towards the cobblestones. She was nervous, I thought. Well, I supposed that was to be expected. The first and only time she had met Mr. Holmes had been when he had assisted in solving the murder of Mr. Wickham, a time when he was rather abrupt in manner. He had not made a good impression upon anyone except for me.

When we reached the apartment, I first introduced Mary to Mrs. Hudson. Like me, Mary seemed impressed and surprised that a woman could run a business all on her own. She asked after Mr. Hudson, only to learn that he had been hanged some time before.

"Oh, I'm terribly sorry," Mary said, as I once had.

"That was how I met Mr. Holmes, in fact," Mrs. Hudson informed her. "He helped me."

Confusion crossed Mary's face. "He tried to have your husband freed?"

"Oh, no, dear!" Mrs. Hudson beamed. "He ensured he was convicted!"

Mary blinked rapidly in confusion and then looked at me. I couldn't help but laugh. Such had been my reaction once upon a time when I had learned more about Mrs. Hudson. "Come on, Mr. Holmes is upstairs."

I warned her, as we walked up, that the apartment would be in disarray. "I do my best to keep it tidy but if you see something like a skull on the mantelpiece, just take it in your stride. Mr. Holmes is always conducting experiments to occupy his time when he's not on a case."

When I opened the door, however, I had to stop in surprise. Mary was walking behind me and nearly ran into me. "What is it?"

"Mr. Holmes isn't here," I said, surprised.

There was of course the possibility that Mr. Holmes was in the bedroom, an area of the flat that I had yet to visit and didn't intend to now, but whenever he was in the bedroom the door was closed to indicate it. I had long suspected that the bedroom was merely another room to house his many knickknacks, including books stuffed with newspaper clippings and information on various persons of interest. But whenever he was in it for sleeping or for changing into or out of the many disguises he used, the door was closed.

Now, the door was open. Glancing inside I could see clearly that there was no one there.

Where could he possibly be?

"Well, we might as well sit and wait," I said. There was nothing else planned for the day and Mr. Holmes would be by sooner or later.

I sat myself down in the chair by the fire—the second one that Mr. Holmes had recently obtained for my benefit, since his high-backed dark pink chair was for him alone. It was little unspoken things like that which reminded me that Mr. Holmes cared for our acquaintance, no matter how poorly he did at showing it in conventional terms. I shook my head as Mary made to sit down in it and instead looked around for where else she might sit, when the door opened with a bang.

"There you are," I said, turning to look.

It was a good thing that I had become used to Mr. Holmes's fondness for disguising himself, otherwise I should have thrown out the tramp before me at once. "You look like an ungroomed stable hand," I said.

"That is exactly what I intended to look like, Miss Bennet, thank you," Mr. Holmes replied. "Miss Mary, I wondered if I would be seeing you again."

It was nice to know that even Mr. Holmes, with his great powers of observation, could not guess the future. "She has some information that I thought would be of great interest to you," I said, "But perhaps you had better first change."

Mr. Holmes tipped his head to us and disappeared into the bedroom. Mary turned to look at me, and I did not have to have strong powers of observation to read the confusion in her face. "Mr. Holmes has found that when he's pursuing a case, disguising himself as someone he's not can help him to get information, especially now that people are beginning to recognize him for his services."

"That makes sense," Mary said. "It has been some time since I last saw him but had you not addressed him, I never would have known it to be him. He carries himself in an entirely different manner and his face was all but obscured."

"He's quite clever at it," I replied. "I've often wished to try it myself, but so far my position as a daughter of a gentleman has been more helpful than disguising myself as, say, a maid."

Mr. Holmes emerged, now cleaned and dressed in his usual manner with his pipe already in hand. I suspected that he kept it on him at all times, even when in disguise, perhaps in his pocket. "You said that Miss Mary might have something of interest to me?" He said, never one to worry about pleasantries when there was a task at hand.

I explained what Mary had told me so far. "I stopped her there, thinking she should tell you the rest in person."

Mr. Holmes's eyes brightened in that feverish way they had when he scented another part of the puzzle was coming together. "Yes, I'd be grateful if she'd finish telling us what she knows."

"I'm afraid I don't know much more," Mary replied. "Only what I have managed to sketch out in eavesdropping upon the men. It seems that this Moriarty finds some way to obtain powerful information. How he goes about it, no one can figure out. Personally, I suspect he uses the servants."

"A clever deduction," Mr. Holmes said. "I myself use the homeless to gather information, but most people overlook people who are lower down the ladder than themselves."

"However he does it," Mary explained, "He manages to get information that is extremely sensitive, either personal information or government information. It's starting to become a bit of an open secret, which doesn't surprise me, nobody could operate on such a level while remaining completely unknown. But he's not someone that others like to talk about. They say he has spies everywhere, but I think they also fear the embarrassment. Who wants to be the one who gossiped and admitted that, say, the English government is being blackmailed by a supposed master criminal? It's highly embarrassing."

"And then those in power, fearing their private scandals or political machinations will be brought to the public eye, pay him in whatever he pleases, whether it's information or money," Mr. Holmes finished. "Yes, I see. Very clever of him."

"From what I've heard, sometimes his demands are strange," Mary said, "Or at least they're strange to some of the men. But I've noticed that many of his demands end up turning the tide of political issues, such as aiding or destroying a small rebellion in one country or another. I think his aim isn't wealth but rather he likes being in power. He likes changing history."

"Ah, so he is a megalomaniac," Mr. Holmes intoned. "Someone who is obsessed with his own importance and power."

"It appears so." Mary nodded her agreement.

"Given that Mr. Holmes has been increasingly asked by higher members of society to assist them," I said, "It would make sense that Moriarty would want to intimidate you or possibly get rid of you altogether so that you won't interfere with his plans later on."

Mr. Holmes nodded his agreement. "You have been most helpful, Miss Mary. Perhaps while your sister and I work on our current case you would write down all that you have heard, in as much detail as possible, so that I can add it to my wall?" He indicated the massive wall of information he had obtained about Moriarty so far.

Mary nodded. "I would be happy to help in any way that I can."

"What is there to work on for the current case?" I said, for in telling him about Mary's knowledge I had also told him of Miss Adler. "It has something to do with your disguise and where you were just now, no doubt."

"As observant as ever," Mr. Holmes replied. "Yes, today I went out and disguised myself, as you accurately noted, as a stable hand. I learned of Miss Adler's address from one of my homeless agents, and so went down to offer my services grooming the horses of the various carriages down there. They were happy to have my help, for it was in a very busy and fashionable district.

"In chatting with the other grooms I learned much about Miss Adler. For instance, she is called upon at least once a day, often twice, by a local barrister by the name of Godfrey Norton."

"A barrister," I said. "Then could it be that she's entrusted the portrait to him?"

"It's possible," Mr. Holmes replied. "But if so, he would not need to call upon her so frequently, as he has done apparently for the past six months."

"Then I should think their relationship is personal in nature," I said. "I would dare say she is his friend, or perhaps even more than his friend."

"We are in agreement," Mr. Holmes said. "In my expertise, women tend to keep their secrets close to them, is that true?"

"It has been my experience," I said. "Women and men like to gossip with the secrets of others, but when it comes to their own secrets, I've found most women prefer silence."

"Then it must be somewhere in her house," Mr. Holmes declared. "And if that is the case, then we must find where it is hidden."

"But how?" I asked.

"I have an idea," Mr. Holmes said, getting that gleam in his eyes that happened when he had a plan in mind but did not yet wish for me to know it. "I only ask two things of you: that you call upon Miss Adler this afternoon, and that after certain things occur—you will know them when they happen—that you then go outside and yell 'fire' at the top of your voice."

"Very well," I said. "But I shall expect some surprise or other is up your sleeve."

"And you are wise to do so," Mr. Holmes replied, and his smile was nothing short of conspiratorial.

Chapter Five:
Holmes and the Woman

I called upon Miss Adler as Mr. Holmes wished, that very afternoon. It was impudent to call too late in the day for then it would be seen by the hostess as angling for an invitation to dinner—an intimate honor reserved only for the most revered of guests and intimate acquaintances.

Despite Mr. Holmes's assurances, I personally was concerned that Miss Adler might discover the true reason for my visit. The fact that I myself wasn't sure how I would find out the location of the picture was of little consequence—I knew this woman to be clever and that was enough to worry me. Many men may underestimate the intelligence of women, but I was an intelligent woman myself and knew better than to think Miss Adler a pretty face and nothing more.

Miss Adler, however, received me with great kindness. "I wanted only to thank you again," I said, "And to tell you that your scheme has worked wonders. I am quite left alone now and can pursue honorable men."

"I am glad to hear it," Miss Adler replied, ringing for some tea. "Please, stay and take some refreshments. I confess I have been wanting to know more about you since our meeting last night."

We talked for some time, and I found her to be an engaging and—as I had already suspected—intelligent woman. She was very well-read and educated on a number of subjects, and far more worldly than I, who had never been out of England. She still spoke with traces of an American accent, but years of singing opera in French, Italian, and German had muddled it. I had not had many occasion to meet people from the former colonies, but when I did, I found their accents to be bothersome to my ear. Miss Adler's was sufficiently diluted to be pleasing.

I confessed to her my feeling of inferiority, having traveled not at all and certainly not as knowledgeable on the classics and art. Miss Adler only replied that I was quick witted and eager to learn, and that was all it took to make a pleasant conversationalist.

"To be honest," I said, "I cannot find it in me to be drawn to any man. I have recently found myself a profession, and although I should think most would not approve, it fulfills me as I fear a marriage would not. I'm sure that you feel the same way about your artistry."

"I do and I do not," Miss Adler told me in return. "I love my art and I shall continue it, but I have longed for a life companion, someone to properly share myself with." She leaned in and lowered her voice in a gesture of conspiracy. "I have found myself a proper gentleman recently, one that I dare say I might soon be joined with."

This was a twist to the plot. Of whom could she be speaking, I wondered. "What is he like?"

"He is a proper man, one who respects me despite the ups and downs that my life has seen fit to throw at me, and the fact that I act upon the stage." Miss Adler pulled a face. "There is a common conceit that all actors are made to sin, even those who act upon grand stages or perform great works of art such as opera."

"It is rather hypocritical," I agreed, "That people should enjoy your art and pay to see you perform, but then scorn you and your lifestyle. It is for your art that they love you and yet they claim it makes you a sinner."

"Precisely." Miss Adler nodded. "And as I hinted before, it has made me a target. Many men of consequence have seen fit to try and win me over, thinking that I will give them what they want without fuss and be content to play their mistress. Why should I, when I know full well it will only give them power over me and they can never make me their proper wife? It will only ruin me—and I have loved none of them powerfully enough to embrace that ruin."

"But now you have found someone," I prompted.

"Yes. He is not as high class as some of those who have pursued me, but he is a good man. That is all that I want at this stage. You would do well to find one yourself."

"I'm afraid that I don't want to tie myself to someone," I said. "Especially if they would prevent me from doing my work."

"But you will need protection," Miss Adler replied. "It is wise to have a backup plan."

"Now you begin to sound like my mother," I said, but I was laughing, for there was no judgment in Miss Adler's tone as there was in my mother's.

"I am all for your profession, whatever it may be," said Miss Adler. "I only think it is smart for a woman to have a safety net of sorts, in case the worst should happen. Unfortunately, in our times, that safety net is often a man."

I could see her wisdom in saying so, although my pride struggled with the idea. I did not wish to be bound to anyone, especially someone I did not love—or even if I did love them, the idea of marrying them only to secure my own protection felt a little as though I was using them.

However, there was one good that was coming out of this conversation: I was beginning to suspect that Miss Adler's frequent visitor was not merely her lawyer or friend, but rather her intended. I felt that clenching, sick feeling in my stomach as guilt settled and I realized that Mr. Holmes and I had both assumed the worst of their relationship and that Miss Adler would give into intimacy with a man before marriage in such an easy manner.

"Has he made you a proper proposal?" I asked, just to be certain.

"We have skirted around the matter," Miss Adler replied. "But he comes to me at least once a day, and he is always bringing me gifts or having flowers sent to be waiting for me in my dressing room after a show. If he is not intending marriage, then I think he would have given up by now, sine I have made it clear that all he shall get from me is smiles and conversation."

"Your resolve does your character proud, for I have known women to give sway with much less persuasion than that," I said, thinking of the few women I had heard of—spoken about in whispers—who had allowed a handsome face and pretty words to sway them. Mr. Wickham, for example, was one such a man. He had seduced Miss Bingley, nearly persuaded Miss Georgiana to marry him, and briefly ensnared Lydia before he tried to take too much too soon. Goodness knew how many other women he had ensnared over the years before his untimely death.

It struck me that I was facing a woman of singular character. She had gone through a challenging career on her own as a woman, one where she was constantly fighting against other women for the lead roles, and derided by the common public as someone inclined towards sin. Actors of all kinds were considered among the lower classes, with perhaps only women who waited in brothel houses to be lower. Many actresses, I am sure, gave into temptation and allowed themselves to be wooed by monarchs and nobility and other powerful men in order to receive some kind of money and stability. They got to hang on their arms for a few weeks and enter into their intimate parties and dinners, and feel on top of the world.

But all of that ended, eventually, and those women were left with nothing. Miss Adler had seen this and had endured, and now it seemed that she had found herself a man who was worthy of her character. I had to admire her for it.

I said as much, and Miss Adler thanked me, looking for the first time a bit like a schoolgirl as she blushed beneath my praise. I resolved to tell Mr. Holmes that perhaps we ought to leave the lady alone—but there was the matter of her threat to the king. I still did not understand that, for it seemed out of character for the woman sitting in front of me. Perhaps as we talked I should discover more.

From there our conversation moved on to such subject as literature and art. She recommended to me some books, and after delaying as much as I could, I found that I had to depart, without having learned anything more of value to us.

I was honestly sad to have to leave. With my dear Jane caught up with her baby, and Charlotte far away and only reachable by letter, I had been lonely in the way of companionship. Mr. Holmes was a good friend and he filled my life with excitement and purpose, but he was not the sort of man with whom I could sit and talk. Miss Georgiana, although delightful, was younger than I, and a better companion for Kitty and Lydia than for me. Miss Adler with her education and intelligence made for someone I would wish to call a friend, if only circumstances had been different.

After bidding my farewells I had just stepped out into the lane again when I found myself rushed into by a rude gentleman. I was astonished, even more so when I felt him grabbing for my purse. I reared backwards, hanging onto it, but the gentleman's hand was also firm—and then a second gentleman, an older member of the clergy, was there and assisting me in beating off the ruffian.

Unfortunately, the other man struck a blow that quite felled the clergyman. I gave a cry as blood began to flow freely down the poor man's face.

You can well imagine my surprise when I bent down and peered into the face of Mr. Holmes!

I knew at once that I could not give him away, and instead gave quite a hew and cry about the "poor gentleman who had assisted me."

Miss Adler, as I expected, came out at once, and was equally appalled at the treatment the clergyman—secretly Mr. Holmes—had received.

"Oh, we must bring him inside," I said. "He's still breathing, perhaps he only needs some rest?"

Miss Adler agreed at once, and with some help from the manservants we were able to carry Mr. Holmes inside and lay him upon a couch in the sitting room. In doing so, Mr. Holmes pressed his hand to mine, and I was able to take from it a small sort of bag in which I knew had previously been the blood that had become smeared on his face. I secreted it in my purse as we arranged him.

I must admit I felt great pangs of guilt at what we were doing when I saw how tenderly Miss Adler attended to him. Mr. Holmes had made himself look quite a bit older and Miss Adler was full of concern for the older clergyman, helping to clean up his face and providing him with tea. I quickly made my excuses, feigning sickness at the blood, and retreated from the room. I had to remind myself that for us to not go through with our plan now would only make us look foolish, and we had made a promise and must carry that promise through with honor.

There was a window into the sitting room, which when I exited I went to stand outside of. The window had been opened so that Mr. Holmes might get some "fresh air" to help with his recovery. I stood there and waited, and after a minute or two, Mr. Holmes gave me a signal with his hand.

I cried out at the top of my lungs, "Fire! Oh heavens, fire! Fire!" I then threw through the window a small device, which Mr. Holmes had called a smokerocket. He had given it to me on the walk over—it was an ingenious little device, with a cap on each end to make it self-lighting. Once I threw it in it began to smoke. I then hurried away, and walked up and down the street a bit, waiting for my companion.

There was some measure of curiosity plaguing me as I waited. This was the first time that Mr. Holmes and Miss Adler had met. What should they think of one another? Would Miss Adler seize upon our plan? Would she know that I was involved?

After about ten minutes or so, Mr. Holmes approached me—or rather an older clergyman approached me, the blood on his face now cleaned up. "A resounding success," he said, smiling with pride at himself.

I might be a victim to pride myself at times, but so is Mr. Holmes. It is part of why we understand one another and also part of why we argue with such frequency. Privately, I thought that perhaps his pride should soon take a fall. "Do you have the portrait then?"

"No, but I know where it is hidden."

"And how did you manage that?" I asked, greatly surprised. "She would not have told you." I had spoken with Miss Adler at length upon the subject of my supposed issue, and she had not told me where her portrait was, so why should she show it to a clergyman?

"No, but she did show me." Mr. Holmes smiled. "When you let out the cry of fire, which was soon taken up by others, what did the lady do? What any sensible person does—she dashed for the most valuable thing in her house. Your sister Mrs. Bingley would no doubt have run to her baby, and your sisters Miss Kitty and Miss Lydia for their favorite jewels. Miss Adler reacted much more calmly than I have seen any other woman react in such a situation. She quickly and calmly went to the bell-pull—there is a recess behind a sliding panel there. The photograph is in there. When I cried out that it was a false alarm she replaced it, saw the rocket, and left the room without a word."

"Then we must fetch this photograph!"

"I am to do so tomorrow," Mr. Holmes replied.

"But she might have moved it by then," I said. "You should take care not to underestimate her, Mr. Holmes, for she is a clever woman. Do not think I am the only one of our sex out there who can match wits with you."

As I said this, we had reached the front door for Mr. Holmes's flat. He was just getting his keys out to unlock it, for Mrs. Hudson was out, when we heard the voice of a young man.

"Good afternoon, Mr. Sherlock Holmes!"

We both turned. That voice was familiar to me—yet I saw no one on the street that I recognized. There were several young men about the street—and it must have been one of them, for though masculine, it was not deep enough to belong to someone with a large chest like Mr. Darcy, or of advanced age such as my father. How odd.

"I have heard that voice before," Mr. Holmes remarked. "I wonder who that could have been."

If Mr. Holmes could not easily place the person, then I didn't see how I could. Instead I followed him in, wondering all the while.

Chapter Six:
Holmes is Thwarted

The next day I went early to Baker Street, leaving my sisters again unattended. I was too eager to hear from Mr. Holmes about the photograph to wait a moment longer, and I was certain that at any point he should come bursting through the front door with it in hand.

When I arrived I asked Mrs. Hudson, who indeed informed me that as I had suspected Mr. Holmes had gone out, but had left a message for me saying all was going according to plan and that if I could wait for him, he should return shortly.

I took some tea with Mrs. Hudson, who was eager to tell me all the gossip going on in the neighborhood. Much of it was what even my mother would have deemed too scandalous, such as children born out of wedlock, divorces, and the like, but it fascinated me. Here right under my nose there had been the entire time this whole other world, one that I had never even properly considered until this moment. It made me think of Sarah and Mrs. Hill, two of the servants we had long employed at Longbourn. What sort of troubles and triumphs had they experienced in their lives that I had never even noticed?

Furthermore—and I admit this with some shame—Mrs. Hudson was, to me, almost a replacement for my mother. I loved my mother, but we had never been close. I had never felt that I could go to her with my troubles and hopes the way that my sisters could. Jane and I had taken council with one another instead, or I had written to my dear aunt, Mrs. Gardner, who often accompanied me to balls in London so that we might more easily chaperone the three girls.

I could not, however, admit all that I was experiencing with Mr. Holmes to my aunt. She was an adventurous woman but busy with her own children, being only a few years older than myself and Jane, and I feared that her adventurousness would not extend quite so far. Mrs. Hudson, however, was my mother's age, and had seen much darker things than what I had experienced with Mr. Holmes. I felt that I could tell her anything and she would accept it with a cheery grace.

Despite my enjoyment of my time with Mrs. Hudson, however, after some time I had to observe that it was taking Mr. Holmes much longer than it should have to return. "I hope that he has not been waylaid," I said, glancing at the clock, for it was now almost noon.

There came a knock at the door—and at first I thought it was Mr. Holmes, although I saw no reason why he should knock when he had his own key—but then Mrs. Hudson opened it to reveal my sister Mary.

I stood up. "Whatever is the matter?" I asked, only realizing afterwards that I had done the same to her as she had done to me yesterday, assuming that one of us should only wish to speak to the other if something was wrong.

Mary looked as though she had run here. "A letter came for you," she said, trying to catch her breath. She held it out to me. "From a Miss Adler. She wishes for you to meet her at the Church of St. Monica in the Edgeware Road at noon. She said it was most urgent!"

I took the letter and read it quickly, seeing that it said the same as what Mary had told me. I was at once worried for the fate of Mr. Holmes, and of any other developments that I could not even begin to guess the nature of.

"Look after Mary, would you Mrs. Hudson?" I asked, fetching my shawl. "I must go at once."

I hurried as fast as I was able, grateful that the church in question was not far from Baker Street. Nor was it far from Miss Adler's home, I noted, as I hurried up the steps.

Inside a strange sight greeted me. I had not known fully what I expected when I entered the church, but it was something of the nature of Miss Adler alone, or perhaps with Mr. Holmes, seated upon a pew perhaps. What I did not at all expect was Miss Adler in what was most likely her best dress, with a handsome man standing beside her, and a clergyman—all at the altar!

There was a fourth person standing with them, a man with the kind of red nose that indicated a long-standing drinking habit and ill-fitting clothes. As I hurried up to the altar I observed the look in his eyes and the way he held himself, and then saw, in his coat pocket, the outline of a pipe.

Mr. Holmes was here as well? Would wonders never cease? I considered, for a moment, the idea of the universe playing some great trick on me, and that these two had conspired together to make a joke of me—would the king now step out and expose himself as well?

But when I reached them, Miss Adler took hold of my hands and wrung them gratefully. "I am so glad you could make it," she said, "For indeed I have no other friend in the world who I could trust, and who was in London at this time."

"I am grateful that you trust me so," I said, "But I'm quite confused as to what is happening."

Miss Adler gestured to the handsome young man, perhaps a year or two older than myself. "This is Mr. Norton, a man that I hope shall in the next few minutes become the person to whom I will tie my life. He is a most honorable man, Miss Bennet, but there is a bit of trouble with our license. We are in need of two witnesses before we can make it legal, and it must happen before noon."

"I was able to fetch this gentleman," Mr. Norton said, gesturing at Mr. Holmes. "He was loitering outside the church and no doubt had a lack of anything better to do. I pulled him in here, I fear in quite a rush, he must think me mad."

"Only until you explained yourself, sir," Mr. Holmes replied, his voice thick and bearing a different accent than usual.

"Now that we are all assembled," the clergyman said, "We can begin."

And so it was that Mr. Holmes and I stood witness to the marriage of Irene Adler to Godfrey Norton—an event that I confess I did not even conceive as a possibility. I suppose that I must have seen it coming, for when a man calls upon a woman as frequently as Mr. Norton called upon Miss Adler, there was something afoot. But to my shame, I only considered her his mistress, and not the woman he was lawfully marrying. In doing so I had assumed much ill of both Mr. Norton and Miss Adler, and silently asked that my standing witness to their union be my form of penance for that.

After the vows were said and it was all done in the matter of an instant, I heard the church bells ringing to announce noon. Miss Adler and Mr. Norton both breathed a heavy sigh of relief.

"It should not have been legal had we not got it in before then," Mr. Norton confessed.

Miss Adler—but then, she was Mrs. Norton now—smiled at me and gave me a hug. "Thank you, dear creature!" She cried out, and I felt guilt settle in upon my stomach again. "You have helped to make me the happiest woman in the world."

Mr. Holmes, still in character, wandered out of the church on his own, but I was obliged to properly meet and greet Mr. Norton, and inquire after his health, and learned that he met his now-wife when she needed representation renegotiating her contract with the opera house.

"They were using her most shamefully," Mr. Norton said, and I noted the protectiveness and admiration in his voice as he looked upon his wife. "I know she is not a soprano, they generally get all the praise, but such a rare voice and such a fine one! They knew they needed her and yet they thought she was not aware of it and would let them bully her. I soon set that to rights."

"We are departing for the continent," Mrs. Norton told me. "But when I return, if I am still welcome to your heart, Miss Bennet, I should gladly like to continue our acquaintance and see if we cannot make an attempt at a real friendship."

I told her that nothing would please me more, and saw them off in a carriage. Upon their leaving, Mr. Holmes sidled up to me.

"What on earth was that?" I cried out, gesturing at the disappearing carriage. "They are leaving even now for the continent!"

"She cannot take the picture with her," Mr. Holmes replied. "If her husband should find it, it would turn their marriage into a shamble. Even a man such as that would not be entirely understanding."

"I should think not, for you are not so forgiving yourself, and you have no interest in her," I replied, a little piqued on Mrs. Norton's behalf.

"Then the photograph will still be in her apartment," Mr. Holmes said. "We must hurry!"

We did not at first go to the apartment, as I had thought—instead, Mr. Holmes went with me and we called upon the rooms which the king had told us he had rented out, and where we could leave notice for him. Mr. Holmes instructed a letter to be sent, and after a short while, during which time I got myself some lunch, for I had not eaten properly that day, our client greeted us.

He was wearing plain clothing that I thought he might have taken from a servant, and wore a hat which he kept low over his eyes. A few little touches changed his appearance, such as added sideburns and a mustache. I wanted to laugh, for I thought it comical that he try and alter his appearance, for I could still recognize him—but I thought it would be rude of me to say so.

"You have it, then?" he asked, and the hope in his eyes was so great that for a moment I was sorry to contradict him.

"Not yet," Mr. Holmes said, "But we know where it is. Come, we must make haste."

We hurried to Mrs. Norton's apartment, where Mr. Holmes was easily able to charm the maidservant into letting us in. I had found that when it is required to gain information for a case, Mr. Holmes could be quite persuasive.

We entered the sitting room, only to find that something lay in wait for us there: a picture of Mrs. Norton, and a letter, addressed to Mr. Holmes... and Miss Bennet.

My breath caught in my throat. So my association with Mr. Holmes had become discovered. I looked at Mr. Holmes in surprise and dismay, wondering what the letter contained.

"What is this?" the king asked, equally as astonished as I was.

Mr. Holmes caught up the letter. "I believe that if we read this, we shall find out."

Chapter Seven:
A Pity

Mr. Holmes read the letter silently to himself, and then out loud. I was glad to hear it, for at the moment my hands were trembling so much that I could not have picked it up to read it myself. I felt great shame, and also the fool, for I had not once suspected that Miss Adler in her kind demeanor knew of my deceit.

The letter read as follows:

My dear Mr. Holmes and Miss Bennet,
You really did it very well. You took me in completely. Until the alarm of a fire, I had not a single suspicion. You might consider a career upon the stage, the both of you, especially in regards to disguises, Mr. Holmes.

But then, after I had revealed myself, I knew at once that I had been betrayed in some manner. The nature of Miss Bennet's assistance I confess I did not at once guess, but I had been warned of you, Mr. Holmes, some months ago by the same person who paid me to threaten the king with the publication of his portrait.

I know that it ate at you so, wondering why I should threaten him with it—especially, as I'm sure Miss Bennet could tell you, I did not love him and never have. Why, in that case, should I threaten him with such dishonor?

I am not sure how this gentleman came to know of the existence of the portrait. He suggested to me that he knew of it through the letters that I had sent to the king, which were still in the king's possession and this gentleman somehow got a hold of and read. I was paid a good sum, and asked only that I threaten the king with this exposure. But I was warned that the king might employ you, Mr. Holmes, and that I should be on the lookout against you. Your address at Baker Street had even been given to me.

And yet, even armed with this, you still caused me to reveal what you wanted to know. The psychology of the mind is such a fascinating thing, is it not? In that moment, with the cry of fire, all I could think of was that I must save my one protection against a powerful man who could destroy me if he so chose. That is what powerful men do to loose ends, after all, and only that portrait saves me.

For a moment, I did not want to believe that it was you. I hated to think evil of such a kind clergyman, one who had been attacked for helping such a dear lady as Miss Bennet. But it must be you, and if so, then you must have employed Miss Bennet as well. It came to me that it was too great of a coincidence that Miss Bennet should appear in my dressing room with a story so like mine, and then be so eager to make a friendship with me. I hope, Miss Bennet, that not all of your cheer was faked, and I am in earnest when I say that I wish our friendship to be renewed someday. But more on that later.

I have been trained as an actress myself, Mr. Holmes, as you are well aware. While I hated to suspect it, I knew that I must know for certain. The moment I left the room I sent my coachman, a loyal man who has been with me some time, to watch you, while I dashed upstairs to change into some walking-

clothes that I have kept about me. I have played a man before, as Miss Bennet may tell you, for dressing women up in the disguise of men is a common plot device in the opera, especially with my lower voice.

I came down just as you departed and followed you—and there I saw you reuniting with Miss Bennet. I followed you to your home on Baker Street, and there, foolish as it was, I could not resist calling out to you

The young man who had wished us goodnight! I realized that was why he had sounded so familiar to us—we had both at that point heard Miss Adler speak on numerous occasions. But she had disguised her voice so cleverly, as only one who spends every day training and manipulating their voice can, that although it struck us as familiar we could not place it as her. I could not even place it as a woman—I had truly thought a young man had spoken.

I could see by his face that Mr. Holmes was thinking along the same lines that I was. After a moment, he shook himself, and returned to finishing the letter.

After wishing you a good afternoon so impudently, I hurried to see the man that I now call my husband. I doubt that either of you will understand what it means to trust someone so completely, but I had long ago told him of my misfortunes with your royal client. I relayed to him what had happened that day, and he was in support of the idea that flight was the best option.

I will have told Miss Bennet that we are going to the continent, but that is not true. We are setting sail for the Americas, where I am contracted to do a tour of concerts around the country, and a few operas in New York City. Miss Bennet will have to forgive the deception—I thought that if it were known where we were truly going, there might be agents at the ports to stop us.

And then the wedding! I admit that was great fun on my part. I knew, Mr. Holmes, that you should follow me and see when best to take the portrait from me, so I led you to the chapel. Miss Bennet as well, for I do truly desire her company and we were in need of a second witness. The look of complete surprise upon your face in that moment, Miss Bennet, when you saw us up on the altar, is something I shall treasure for some time. It is not easy to fool such formidable opponents as you two. You must allow me to congratulate myself, just a little.

And so when you arrive at my house after the wedding, you will find it empty. The birds have flown the nest. As for the photograph, your client can rest in peace. I love and am loved by a better man than he. The king may do what he will without hindrance from one he has so cruelly wronged. I keep it only to safeguard myself, and to preserve a weapon which will always secure me from any steps which he might take in the future.

I leave a photograph which he might care to possess. My dear Miss Bennet, I remain your friend, and hope you shall accept the gifts from the Americas I am sure to send you.

As for my dear Mr. Sherlock Holmes, I remain, very truly yours,

Mrs. Irene Norton, nee Adler.

I stared in shock as Mr. Holmes finished reading the letter. She had figured us out so thoroughly! She had known exactly what we were doing and what we should do! I felt completely played for a fool—and a bit so by Mr. Norton as well, in only that I had underestimated his generosity of spirit in understanding his wife's history.

Mr. Holmes seemed to be in a similar state of surprise and stared down at the letter for some time. I had never known Mr. Holmes to be bested before, and so I think it rather hit him harder than it hit me. I had been bested by Mr. Holmes, for one, and had been shown on several occasions that I could overestimate myself and miscalculate others.

The king, meanwhile, was in a sort of surprise as well, but a much more pleased on. I should have thought he would be greatly upset but instead he was laughing. I felt like he would start applauding at any moment.

"What a woman!" he cried. "Oh, what a woman!" He gestured me and Mr. Holmes, then at the letter. "Did I not tell you how quick-witted she was? How resolute her temperament?" He sighed, and his eyes took on a far-off look, as if he were daydreaming. "Would she not have made an admirable queen? It is a pity she is not on my level?"

I had quite a few remarks that I could say to that, none of them flattering and quite a few enough to land me in a pot of trouble, but Mr. Holmes spoke before my temper could.

"From what I have seen of the lady she seems indeed to be on a very different level to your Majesty," Mr. Holmes said, and his tone was as cold and condescending as I have ever heard it. "I am sorry that I have not been able to bring your Majesty's business to a more successful conclusion."

The king waved away Mr. Holmes's concerns. "On the contrary, my dear sir, nothing could be more successful! Did I not tell you earlier that her word is her bond? That was why I was so afraid when she said she would publish, for I knew that she would. But now she speaks that she will not use it, and her word is inviolate. It is as safe now as if it were in a fire."

"I am glad to hear your Majesty say so," Mr. Holmes replied, still rather stiff. It was clear to me that in his behavior, and Miss Adler's own cleverness, Mr. Holmes had come to agree with me about Miss Adler being the injured party here.

I nursed just the slightest bit of pride at knowing that Mr. Holmes had come over to my side of thinking in that matter.

"I am immensely indebted to you," the king informed us. "Pray tell me in what way I can reward you." He paused, and then his eyes lit up. "Perhaps this ring," he said, beginning to draw off his finger a very fine ring, one done in the shape of a snake with emeralds for the pattern along its back.

Mr. Holmes held up a hand to stop him. "Your Majesty has something which I should value even more highly."

I could only wonder what that could be. I had no use for anything. I lived comfortably under the financial support of Mr. Bingley. I could not ask the king, of all people, to arrange marriages for my three sisters.

And he could not reverse time and make my father younger. There was nothing that he could give me.

Mr. Holmes valued material possessions and wealth even less than I did. What did the king have that he could want?

"The first," Mr. Holmes said, "Is that you be honest with me when I ask you if you have heard of a man known as Moriarty. I suspect he is the man that paid Miss Adler to threaten you with the photograph, both to unsettle you and to get you to London for some reason, or to bring me into the matter, or both."

The king sobered at once. "It is true, I have heard of this man. He has previously made himself known to me when he managed to obtain some important state papers, I know not how, from my private chamber. He has cropped up here and there across Europe, but recently his name has been spoken of with more frequency. We are at a loss on how to handle him."

"It seems that he blackmails in exchange for favors of some kind," Mr. Holmes put forth.

"Yes, although the nature of these is often confusing to me."

"I'm sure that they are," Mr. Holmes replied, and I had to stifle a snort of derision. I hoped that the king would not notice the insult to his intelligence, and fortunately for all of our sakes it seemed that he had not. "Thank you for your input, your Majesty. It's greatly appreciated. As for the second thing…"

"Whatever it is, you may name it."

I considered asking for an earldom, if only to see what the king would say in response to that.

"I hope that you won't think me too forward," Mr. Holmes said, with an uncharacteristic attention to manners, "But I should like the photograph."

He indicated the photograph of Irene Adler that had been left behind with her letter. It was a lovely portrait, and in no way scandalous as the king's to Adler's had been. It showed the lady sitting on a lovely sofa, wearing what appeared to be a stately costume from one of her operas.

"Irene's photograph?" The king was puzzled, as was I. I suppose that the king perhaps thought Mr. Holmes had feelings for Miss Adler. But I, knowing this was not Mr. Holmes's way, was completely lost. "Certainly, if you wish it."

He passed the photograph to Mr. Holmes, who carefully pocketed it without even stopping to examine it more closely. My confusion continued.

"I hope," I said, "that you will honor the lady's wishes and not seek her out or bother her with undue attention."

"Certainly not," the king replied. "I have learned the error of my ways in dealing with a woman as clever as that. She shall have no fear of reprisal from me."

I noted that this was not a promise that he should not stray, but I said nothing. My personal judgment I was free to think on in my own mind, but to speak them aloud to the king I had no doubt would only cause problems for us.

"I thank your Majesty," Mr. Holmes said. He bowed, and I curtsied. It amazed me a little, for just a few days before I had fallen to my knees in confusion and in my eagerness to not give offense. Now, in the presence of this same member of royalty, I was calm and collected. What a difference just a little bit of exposure could make!

"Well then," Mr. Holmes said. He looked at me. "Then there is no more to be done in the matter. I have the honor of wishing you a good afternoon."

Mr. Holmes turned away—even as the king stretched out his hand to with which he intended, I've no doubt, to shake Mr. Holmes's hand. I bit hard on the inside of my cheek to stifle a gasp of surprise, and then a laugh, for when Mr. Holmes decided he did not respect someone, there was little he cared to do to hide it.

I followed him out the door. It was fairly obvious to me that the king wasn't about to accept shaking my hand. He hadn't even looked at me properly or spoken to me, unless I spoke first, throughout the entire exchange. I might have been Mr. Holmes's associate and that was enough to get most people to address me with respect but I suppose that for some people, high enough up in the world, the opinion of someone—even someone as intelligent as Mr. Holmes—was not enough to dissuade them when they wanted to look down on someone.

Yes, I thought, as I hurried to catch up with Mr. Holmes. A pity that some people just aren't on the same level as others.

Chapter Eight:
The Last Surprise

"Well," I said, when I had caught up with him. "I must say that if someone were to ask me whoever could possibly be the match to the great Mr. Holmes, I should have said no one. If pressed, I would then say that perhaps, if this Moriarty proves himself, he may prove Mr. Holmes's equal, in time. But of all people to prove herself the better of you..."

For a moment my friend was silent and I feared that I had genuinely hurt his feelings and pressed too hard on the matter. But then Mr. Holmes graced the stones in front of him with one of his small smiles, and I knew that he saw the amusing side of it as I did.

"I have indeed been outsmarted for the first time," he said. "And by a woman."

"You needn't have such a tone of surprise," I said. "Unless you have failed to notice my own gender, in which case, Mr. Holmes, you might be in for a nasty shock."

"Ah, but have you outsmarted me, Miss Bennet?" Mr. Holmes returned. "You have shown remarkable talent and intellect but forgive me for thinking that I was mentoring you."

This was true, and I deflated a little. Mr. Holmes was still more observant than I, and of the two of us I considered him to be the master detective while I was still a bit of an apprentice.

"Chin up, Miss Bennet," Mr. Holmes said. "I'm sure that you will come to outwit me in time and perhaps even surpass me altogether, if this incident is any indication. Such a woman," he added, open admiration in his voice, something I had never before heard from him. "*The* woman."

"Why, Mr. Holmes, I should dare say that you have the more tender feelings for her if I did not know you so well," I said. "Or perhaps, there is a bit of softness lingering in you yet, that even you have not seen fit to acknowledge until now."

"I assure you, Miss Bennet, I have no intention of pining as one of your Gothic heroes or throwing myself into matrimony," Mr. Holmes replied dryly. "But if it entertains you to think of such an amusing scene then by all means, do not let me keep you from your flights of fancy."

I laughed. "Why, you are so offended at the idea of being like ordinary men and women. It is not such a bad thing, or so I hear, to fall in love."

"If so then I wonder that you do not go about it yourself," Mr. Holmes replied. "I am sure that many men would be happy to ask for your hand, if you were to show an interest."

The look on my face undoubtedly betrayed my horror of the idea. Only the deepest of loves could compel me into marriage, especially now that I knew there were so many other options before me. Mr.

Holmes gave a dry chuckle, and I scowled, knowing that he had successfully turned the tables on me.

"On a more serious note," Mr. Holmes said, "Your sister Miss Mary shows an intellect similar to yours and an interest in law and the government."

"Yes," I said. "I was thinking it is a shame that she is not a man. Not that she is not as capable as a man, but now she is barred from what she enjoys because no one would surely let her go to the bar or enter into Parliament."

"As you so astutely noted, I have just now been shown that I should not underestimate a woman," Mr. Holmes said. I saw that he held the photograph of Miss Adler fondly, as one would first prize at a fair. "Perhaps we can set her to some tasks. Organizing my collection of information, for one."

"It is rather haphazard," I said, referring to his system of stuffing books around his flat with newspaper clippings and other information on people about London and the greater world. "I think she shall get an education out of it and enjoy creating order out of the chaos."

"Perhaps next then she can bring some kind of order to my wall," Mr. Holmes added.

I knew that he was referring to his wall plastered with information about Moriarty, for there was no other wall in his flat that held anything of note. "It seems that we are beginning to understand our adversary," I said. "He is someone who likes power and enjoys manipulating governments, either for some greater end or to line his own pockets or even just for the sake of his own amusement."

"Perhaps it is, I think, a combination of all three," Mr. Holmes said. "One may dominate over the others, but I doubt that one rises to such heights and in such a way as this without having a mixture of motives behind them."

"And what are your motives then?" I asked. "You are beginning to rise to prominence yourself, Mr. Holmes. We have had a monarch for a client just this past week, in case you have already forgotten."

"A fool of a monarch indeed," Mr. Holmes said scathingly. "To think at how his behavior has twice, at the least, endangered his country."

"What will become of Miss Adler?" I asked, and then corrected myself. "I mean, Mrs. Norton? That is, she has not and is not going to publish the photograph. Will this Moriarty come after her?"

"Things are done rather differently in America than here in Europe," Mr. Holmes noted. "I do not think Moriarty's sway has gone so far as to reach across the Atlantic. And in any case, Mrs. Norton said only that she was paid to threaten the king with the photograph, not to actually print it. I think Moriarty will let her be."

"I hope so," I said. "I should hate for her to come under fire, so to speak."

"So we are in agreement then?" Mr. Holmes said. "That we shall have Miss Mary as our secretary, of a sort, and help us to compile information about this Moriarty?"

"I suppose," I said. "But I do wish you would be careful to continue to take cases so that you do not slip into obsession. You did worry me a few days ago, Mr. Holmes, as much as I know you hate it when anyone fusses over you."

Mr. Holmes grumbled but I saw that he had a sort of fond look in his eyes. Though he rarely said anything out loud, it was those looks that reminded me that he did indeed see me as a friend and his complaints about me and my 'fussing' were merely for show.

I left Mr. Holmes at his flat in Baker Street, bid a goodnight to Mrs. Hudson, and then made my way home. And so the whole matter of Irene Adler was concluded, at least as far as openly discussing it. But I saw, before I left, that Mr. Holmes was staring most adamantly at her portrait with a look of contemplation that I have rarely seen upon him.

For all of my teasing my friend, I am serious when I share with the reader the fact that Miss Adler, now Mrs. Norton, holds a special place in the annals of history. Her picture was placed upon the mantelpiece, a rare place of honor, in the area formerly occupied by the skull—which I had secretly dubbed Clarence, for those who might have been wondering.

Mr. Holmes had, at times, liked to joke about the cleverness of women. While he felt them capable of intelligence and he certainly never underestimated me, I think that as a whole he was unimpressed by them. He found them flighty and that the average woman was incapable of keeping her head in a crisis. Since

Miss Adler proved him wrong, I have not heard him jest in such a manner.

In a bit of behavior that some may not find so odd given Mr. Holmes's many unusual habits, Miss Adler is the one person that he does not call by name. No, she is special enough to be given a title. To Mr. Holmes she is always 'the woman.' Whenever he refers to her, or even to her picture, it is by that title.

In the years that have past, I have seldom heard him refer to her by any other name. In his eyes she eclipsed and predominated the whole of her sex. I have sincere doubts that Mr. Holmes even remembered that I am a woman as well. To him I have always been his associate, his pupil, and my being a man or a woman was neither here nor there to him. But Irene Adler is *the* woman. She was a representative, I think, to his mind of all that women could be.

As Mr. Holmes had pointed out to me when I teased him, it was not that he felt any emotion akin to love for her. Those tender emotions, and that of romantic love in particular, were abhorrent to his cold, precise but admirably balanced mind. Mr. Holmes was a brilliant man, and one that I admired and considered a friend, but I have to confess that when I pictured him as a lover I only pictured him failing. When he did tend to speak of love it was generally to make a joke of it. They were interesting to observe in others, but he did not care for it.

And yet, there was but one woman to him.

Oh, yes, there was one more thing of note in the adventure of the king's portrait. Many readers might yet be wondering if I managed to maintain my friendship with Mrs. Norton, nee Adler, as she had said she hoped we might upon her return. That was not for some time, but when she eventually made her way back to England, yes, we did strike up a dear and close friendship.

In the meantime it was not long before I received my first letter from her and I was able to respond in kind. I found it heartening that I could have a friendship with someone who was not only my intellectual equal, as Mr. Holmes was, but also a woman, someone with whom I could discuss the warmer things that Mr. Holmes always sneered at.

But the most amusing and interesting thing, Mrs. Norton's last laugh, so to speak, was waiting for me when I arrived back at the Bingley home that evening.

"There is a present for you, Lizzie!" Jane said. She was without the baby for a time, and looked positively radiant. She was not getting much sleep as a new mother but the sheer joy in her face made up for any tiredness about her eyes. I have never seen a woman so in love with her child and her lot in life as a mother as was my Jane.

"A present?" I scoured my mind, trying to think who would have sent such a thing and why. It was not at all near to my birthday, nor could I think of anything I had done that would have earned me a showing of gratitude. Nor did I have any suitors who would leave something for me as a token of affection. Perhaps… "Is it from Aunt Gardner?"

"No, although she did call this morning, she asks that you repay her in kind tomorrow, she misses you," Jane replied. She produced from behind her back a package, wrapped beautifully, with a little ribbon and a small note attached. "It was delivered by a messenger this afternoon while you were out. He said that it was from a friend of yours and to handle it with care."

"I wonder what it could be," I said, equal parts nervous and excited. Could Father have, perhaps, sent me a special book as a surprise? Could Jane herself have arranged this and was pretending not to know anything of it? Or perhaps it was from Charlotte, who was always so thoughtful and sweet?

First, I picked up the note. When I opened it, I gasped and nearly dropped the parcel in shock. "What is it?" Jane asked. "Oh, is it something distressing? You look quite pale, Lizzie."

"It is nothing," I said, "Only that I now know who it is from."

Indeed, I recognized the handwriting at once. I had read another letter written by this person no more than an hour or two ago, left behind on a table with her portrait which now sat on the mantle in Mr. Holmes's flat.

This note had only three words on it: *open in private*.

"I'll open this in my room," I said. "It's from Mr. Holmes for a case, and I have to keep our client private—they're very prominent in society and they've made us promise to be as discreet as possible."

"Oh, of course," Jane replied, and I felt a bit of guilt at lying to her, but that would be nothing compared to the shriek she would undoubtedly let out if she saw what was inside this package. That is, if what was inside the wrapping was what I thought it was. "Dinner will be soon, and then Lydia and Kitty are going to the balls for the night, I presume that you can chaperone them? Charles has agreed if you cannot, but I think he would not have a good time of it—he would have to watch them dancing and you know it's terribly unfair of him to watch when he can't indulge in it himself since I am not there."

"I can chaperone them," I said. "It's of no trouble. But if you'll excuse me, I need to..."

I disappeared up the stairs before I could even finish the sentence, so eager was I to see if I was right in what this package contained.

Once I was in the safety of my room, with the door locked to be certain, I carefully unwrapped the paper wrapping to reveal what was inside.

It was a photograph, in a cabinet frame, with a piece of brown butcher paper carefully placed to cover the undoubtedly scandalous image it contained. There was also another note, done in the same handwriting, upon which was written *for Miss Bennet.*

The first thing I did was find a suitable place to hide the photograph. I did not have a specially made hidden compartment for it, as Miss Adler had, but I was able to successfully hide it by wrapping it inside of a dressing gown that I hardly ever wore and then placing that underneath my intimates. I should find a better hiding place for it later. I had several ideas.

The note I read with eagerness once the picture was securely hidden away.

> *Dear Miss Bennet,*
>
> *I hope you won't think it too forward of me to hide this with you. I think it will be enough for our friend the monarch to simply believe that I have the picture in my possession. I could not risk traveling with it, for if it was lost with my luggage, it would cause a scandal indeed—and while I did happily take the money from the gentleman I previously mentioned, which allowed me to afford this voyage to the Americas in exchange for threatening our blundering king—I do not actually wish my name to be dragged about through the papers in such a fashion.*
>
> *I believe—or perhaps it is that I choose to believe—that you were in earnest in seeking my friendship. I greatly enjoyed our afternoon of discussion and I am grateful for your standing in as a witness at my wedding. I shall write to you shortly when I have a proper address, so that you may respond in kind.*
>
> *Do what you like with the portrait. Burn it, or keep it as insurance, or whichever you see is best. I trust your judgment.*
>
> *Yours sincerely,*
> *Irene*

What could I do to that but laugh? She had managed to surprise me yet again. I did not know what surprised me more: that she should still trust me enough to entrust me this powerful token, or that she should think of the idea of sending it to me in the first place.

What I did with the picture, I shall not say. I think readers can have a guess at it themselves. But the thought that Irene trusted me still even after my abuse of said trust, and the cleverness and joke of her sending the picture to me—it was enough to keep me smiling all throughout the rest of the evening, including while I chaperoned my sisters.

THE END

About the Author

Amelia works as a librarian and lives in an idyllic Cotswold village in England with Darcy, her Persian cat. She has been a Jane Austen fan since childhood but only in later life did she discover the glory and gory of a cozy mystery book. She has drafted many different cases for Holmes and Bennet to solve together.

Visit www.amelialittlewood.com for more details.

Made in United States
Orlando, FL
13 February 2025